With love to Amy, Hannah, Sarah, Jake, Taylor, Grace,
and airport babies around the world. – ED

To Felipe and Francine Andrzejewski, and
Richard Powell; once babies that came from love.
Para Antonia Schwinden, com gratidão, – LNP

And from both author and illustrator, a special
thanks to Kira Lynn and Deborah Warren.

First Edition
Kane Miller, A Division of EDC Publishing

For information contact:
Kane Miller, A Division of EDC Publishing
PO Box 470663
Tulsa, OK 74147-0663

www.kanemiller.com
www.edcpub.com
www.usbornebooksandmore.com

Library of Congress Control Number: 2016950682

Manufactured by Regent Publishing Services, Hong Kong
Printed November 2016 in ShenZhen, Guangdong, China

ISBN: 978-1-61067-557-4

1 2 3 4 5 6 7 8 9 10

BABIES COME FROM AIRPORTS

the ride there

your plane!

YOU!!!!

Kane Miller

A DIVISION OF EDC PUBLISHING

BABIES
COME FROM
AIRPORTS

Written by Erin Dealey

Illustrated by
Luciana Navarro Powell

"Babies come from airports," my brother says, "it's true."

"A big guy named Security let Mommy bring you through."

Dad serves us
warmed-up pizza.
"Don't listen to
your brother.

"Babies come from labor," Dad says.
"Wait and ask your mother."

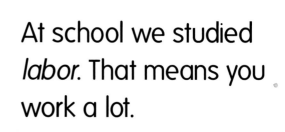

At school we studied *labor*. That means you work a lot.

I bet he means the paperwork took longer than we thought.

I can't ask Mom. She's far away, to meet my baby sister.

I draw Mom lots of pictures so she'll know how much we missed her.

There's one of me at soccer. (I almost scored a goal!)
And one of us pretending that we like Dad's casserole.

I draw one of my brother with gum stuck in his hair. And when the vacuum cleaner sucked my baseball underwear.

Then heading to the airport – my brother,
Dad and me – I draw a *Thank You* picture
for my friend, Security.

"We need to find Security," I whisper to my brother.

"Security! What's wrong, dear?" someone asks me.
"Where's your mother?"

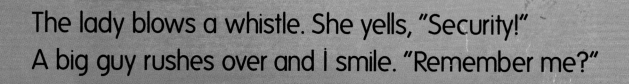

The lady blows a whistle. She yells, "Security!"
A big guy rushes over and I smile. "Remember me?"

Security kneels down. "Don't panic, kid. You'll be OK."
"Stay calm," the lady says.

"We'll find your parents right away."

"My dad's right here," I tell them,
but the woman asks, "You sure?"
"Yes, ma'am," I say as Mommy waves.
"And there's my mom. That's her!"

I show my friend his picture.
"This is us on Gotcha Day. And you bent down and whispered, 'Welcome to the USA.'"

"I'm bigger now," I tell him. He winks and says, "Me too."

"It's Gotcha Day!" cheers Mommy,
as she brings my sister through.

Some babies have a Gotcha. Today's my sister's day.
And when she's big like me, I know exactly what I'll say:

"We met you at the airport. I waved at planes above."
But right now, all she needs to know is . . .

the ride there your plane! you

Babies come from love.